festival of COLORS

written by KABIR SEHGAL & SURISHTHA SEHGAL

illustrated by VASHTI HARRISON

Beach Lane Books • New York London Toronto Sydney New Delhi

Guavas are ripening. Lotuses are blooming.
And Holi, the Indian festival of colors, is almost here.

Chintoo and Mintoo are getting ready.

"HOLI, HAI.

"HOLI, HAI,"

they whisper.

They gather hibiscus flowers,
because hibiscus flowers make

They gather orchids,
because orchids make PURPLE.

They gather marigolds,
because marigolds make ORANGE.

They gather irises,
because irises make BLUE.

Then they lay the flowers out to dry.

Then they separate the petals.

And *then* they press the petals into fine powders.

At last, the petal-powders are ready. Chintoo and Mintoo are ready too!

And so are their parents.

And their friends.

And their neighbors.

And then . . .

POOF!

Purple pops!

POOF!

Red bursts!

POOF!

Orange erupts!

POOF!

Blue splashes!

"Holi, hai! Holi, hai! Holi, hai!" everyone shouts.

Holi is a festival of fresh starts.
And friendship.
And forgiveness.

But for Chintoo and Mintoo,
it's *also* a festival of . . .

A Note from the Authors

Holi is the Indian festival of colors, celebrated during spring, when new colors appear in nature. It symbolizes inclusiveness, new beginnings, and the triumph of good over evil. The festivities begin with an evening bonfire. The next morning, family, friends, and neighbors throw dry and wet colored powders on each other. People chant, "Holi, hai!" which is pronouned, "Holy, heh," and means, "It's Holi!"

Traditionally, the powders were made at home using flowers. Families and friends gathered, dried, and ground the petals into fine powders, which were mixed with water to make brilliant colors. Now most people buy premade powders from the local bazaar or even online.

There is plenty of singing, dancing, and feasting during the festivities. And with everyone covered in vibrant colors, there is a tremendous feeling of community.

To Chris Moses,
who sees all colors and possibilities
—K. S. & S. S.

For my family
—V. H.

BEACH LANE BOOKS • An imprint of Simon & Schuster Children's Publishing Division • 1230 Avenue of the Americas, New York, New York 10020 • Text copyright © 2018 by Surishtha Sehgal and Kabir Sehgal • Illustrations copyright © 2018 by Vashti Harrison • All rights reserved, including the right of reproduction in whole or in part in any form. • BEACH LANE BOOKS is a trademark of Simon & Schuster, Inc. • For information about special discounts for bulk purchases, please contact Simon & Schuster Special Sales at 1-866-506-1949 or business@simonandschuster.com. • The Simon & Schuster Speakers Bureau can bring authors to your live event. For more information or to book an event, contact the Simon & Schuster Speakers Bureau at 1-866-248-3049 or visit our website at www.simonspeakers.com. • Book design by Lauren Rille • The text for this book was set in Avenir. • Manufactured in China • 1218 SCP • 10 9 8 7 6 5 4 3 2 • CIP data for this book is available from the Library of Congress. • ISBN 978-1-4814-2049-5 (hardcover) • ISBN 978-1-4814-2050-1 (eBook)